# The Dog with the Wounded Paw

Buster's tail had started to wag again in anticipation of meeting her.

"Just two more cars," thought Emma, preparing to move. But the impatient dog couldn't wait another second. In one bound Buster was in the road and dashing towards Emma – straight into the path of an oncoming van. Emma squeezed her eyes tight shut, unable to watch the inevitable collision as the van hit Buster. He was tossed into the air, then with an audible thud, fell motionless to the ground.

HIPPO **ANIMAL**

# The Dog with the Wounded Paw

## Brenda Jobling

Hippo

Scholastic Children's Books,
Commonwealth House,
1–19 New Oxford Street,
London WC1A 1NU, UK
A division of Scholastic Ltd
London ~ New York ~ Toronto ~ Sydney ~ Auckland
Mexico City ~ New Delhi ~ Hong Kong

First published in the UK by Scholastic Ltd, 1998

ISBN 0 590 11314 3

Typeset by
Cambrian Typesetters, Frimley, Camberley, Surrey
Printed and bound by Nørhaven Paperback A/S, Denmark

10 9 8 7

For Marisa

# Chapter 1

A tall fourteen-year-old girl, her shoulders weighed down by two heavy school bags, made her way home along a busy North London road. One bag was stuffed full with muddy sports kit, the other groaned under the weight of text books. The girl, Emma Hodges, was wondering which of her homework assignments she should tackle first that evening.

As it was Friday she would try to clear as much of her homework as possible so that she could leave the weekend free – for what she considered to be far more exciting work. Maths, Emma decided, would get first attention. Best to dispense with the one she liked least of all; the others wouldn't seem so bad after that. She hurried on. It would only take another five minutes to reach home.

As Emma passed the last of the railings marking the entrance to her local park, she saw a small group of boys aged from sixteen to eighteen ahead of her. She steeled herself, prepared to ignore any remarks they might throw her way; she'd encountered the group before. It was the biggest member of the group who first spotted her, as he proudly displayed to his friends a new, black leather motorcycle-jacket. Beautifully illustrated on the back in orange, brown and gold paint was a tiger leaping through brilliant green jungle ferns. Beneath the picture, brass studs spelt out the boy's self-appointed name: TIGER.

"Carry your books, Miss?" he asked in a mocking tone, as he leapt to block Emma's path. She ignored him, neatly side-stepping out of his way, to the amusement of the rest of his group. Persisting in his fun, the boy sank to his knees. As Emma passed he implored with affected coyness,

"Oh, *please*! I only want to help you."

Emma struggled to keep her eyes focused straight ahead and continued to walk on – best to ignore them, not say a word. But something suddenly happened which made it impossible for her to stay silent. One of the boys had just lit a cigarette and casually flicked the spent match to the ground. From among the cluster of denim-covered legs, a slim, tan mongrel with soft, silky ears and large, appealing brown eyes emerged yelping and frightened. Emma saw that the short, tatty lead attaching it to the railings was preventing it from moving very far.

"You ought to watch where you throw your matches," she cautioned the boy with the cigarette. "You could have burned that poor dog. As it is, you've scared him witless."

The lad laughed out loud. "Scared! Buster? He's scared of nothing – are you boy?" Five fingers as round and fat as sausages reached to pat the dog's head, but the creature shied away. Emma immediately noticed that it had difficulty in placing one of its front paws on the ground. Dropping her bags, she moved cautiously towards the animal. When it began to wag its tail and attempted to reach her, she slowly extended a hand to comfort it. With confidence, but still wary of an unknown dog, she stroked the creature's head while running her other hand down the leg and gently lifting it to inspect the paw. A tiny fragment of wooden splinter had sunk deep into the pad. Emma took a closer look and decided it was protruding just enough for her to get a grip on it with her nails. With a little assistance from one of the boys to hold the dog steady, she felt she could remove it.

"Could one of you hold on to his collar for me?" she asked the boys who had gathered around. A sixteen-year-old boy with a thin, grey face and lank, straw-coloured hair shuffled forward.

"Buster's *my dog*," he scowled. "What d'you think you're doing to him?"

Emma showed the boy the paw and explained she could probably remove the splinter. It was causing the poor thing unnecessary discomfort. The boy eyed her suspiciously; but she seemed very sure of herself, and he decided to do as she'd requested.

"Get a good grip on that collar, will you?" Emma advised him. Then, steeling herself, she held the paw firmly in one hand while she secured the splinter between the thumb and forefinger of her other hand. "I'm pulling it out – *now*!" she exclaimed.

Much to Emma's relief, all of the splinter came out with one attempt. As it left the fleshy pad, poor Buster yelped and immediately struggled to lick his paw. Emma produced a clean handkerchief from her pocket and dabbed at the oozing wound. As efficiently as was possible while squatting on the pavement of a busy street, surrounded by boys, she bound the hanky around the dog's paw.

The group of boys were dumbstruck. She had worked quickly and competently. Now she knelt comforting Buster, who seemed to have taken a liking to her. "Good, *brave* boy!" She praised him with affection, and he licked the side of her face.

"Well, would you *believe* it!" one of the

boys eventually uttered. "What are you – a vet or something?"

"No," replied Emma, getting to her feet. "But my father is, and, if Buster was my dog, I'd make sure my dad saw him as soon as possible. I've removed all the splinter, but there could be some infection in the pad. Walking on dirty pavements won't help it to heal."

The grey-faced boy who owned the dog shuffled from one foot to the other, stared down at the pavement and muttered, "Look, thanks." He sounded embarrassed. "He must have got that splinter this morning when we were walking on the wasteground. I just hadn't noticed. I'll take care of him now."

Emma looked concerned and persisted: "My dad's clinic is only a little way up the road. You really should bring Buster in for him to take a proper look at that paw. It could become a problem if it's not treated."

The boy continued to appear uncomfortable and failed to meet her gaze. He didn't like to be told what to do.

"Like I said – he'll be all right," he

repeated, and slouched off among the others. Buster stared after Emma, tugging on his lead as if he wanted to stay longer with her.

Emma looked at the dog's big, soft, brown eyes; they were so appealing. She sighed, picked up her bags, and carried on walking with what she hoped looked like confidence. But she soon became aware of the trickle of sweat running down her back, making her school blouse stick to her skin.

"*Why* do I do these things?" she mumbled to herself. "It's like Dad said: I'm much too impulsive. What if that wretched splinter hadn't come out in one go? I really should have fetched Dad to deal with it."

Emma felt relieved when she reached her front door. It always pleased her to see the sign displayed on it: *Dr C R Hodges: Veterinary Surgeon*. Emma often dreamed that one day she would see her own name alongside that of her father. Home, for Emma, was Handley Road Veterinary Clinic where Mr Hodges ran his small, but busy, practice on the ground floor. The two floors above comprised the family's cosy home. She had lived there for as long as she could remember and it housed some of her happiest memories. Sometimes it was difficult to distinguish between home life and the veterinary practice; they were both so much a part of one another. The smell of animals mixed with the odour of disinfectant had always drifted up to pervade the rest of the house. It was on her father's clothes, too, as he dashed in and out attending home visits and emergency calls, when he wasn't in his surgery.

Happily for Emma, much of her life centred around caring for animals. Ever since she had been a very young girl, her greatest ambition had been to become a vet like her father. Saturday mornings, school holidays and even after school – providing her homework had been done – Emma could often be found observing Mr Hodges in his surgery. She wasn't actually allowed to help treat the animals, but she could watch most of the procedures. Emma's appointed role lay in welcoming patients and their sometimes very nervous owners into her father's surgery. From the tiniest Russian hamster to the biggest St Bernard, she was always ready to step in and offer comfort to most of the animals she led in from the waiting room. Most, that is, with the exception of Hubert the tarantula. One glimpse of Hubert, stomping up and down on his massive, hairy legs, had sent Emma fleeing out of the door and halfway along Handley Road. For a moment, she had seriously doubted her ability to become a vet and care for all kinds of creatures. With relief she had greeted the news that Hubert had been referred on for specialist treatment elsewhere.

As Emma got ready for bed that night she wondered how Buster was faring. She worried he might be cowering in pain somewhere – although she doubted it. His strange, sullen-faced owner appeared to really care about him. The look of deep concern on the boy's face, as the splinter had left Buster's pad, told her that much. Before she fell asleep that night, she wished he could see the sense of bringing his dog to see her father.

# Chapter 2

"It's Colin – my mouse – Mr Hodges. He's had babies!"

A bright-eyed eight-year-old boy, who was small for his age, stood framed in the entrance to Christopher Hodge's surgery. The tall, smiling vet adopted a bemused look of concern.

"Well, Casey, stranger things have happened. Let's take a look inside that old shoe box, shall we?"

It was Saturday morning; Emma's favourite day. Homework had been attacked the previous evening. "Now, down to some *real* work," she'd thought as she led Casey, clutching his shoe box, to the examination table. Emma helped the boy untie the string around the box, which was pierced with air-holes. Cautiously, Mr Hodges, Emma and Casey peered inside. A small, white mouse with eyes that glowed like brilliant, red traffic-lights, twitched its whiskers and blinked at the sudden light flooding its temporary home. Close to Colin in soft, clean cotton-wool and sawdust were five tiny pink blobs; each one not much bigger than a thumb nail. Five baby mice lay sleeping soundly. Mr Hodges took a closer look at the little creatures and smiled. Emma had a quizzical look on her face until her father pronounced: "No problems there, Casey. Mother and babies are doing fine. The only thing wrong with Colin is possibly the name — he's a she!" He smiled reassuringly at the boy and replaced the lid on the old box.

"*But*," insisted Casey indignantly, "the girl at school who sold me the mouse said Colin was a *he*!" He looked thoughtful for a moment, then smiled as he congratulated himself: "S'pose I got quite a good deal — a lot more mouses for the price of one!" He looked very pleased with himself.

"Mice," corrected Emma, whispering in his ear. "Lots of 'mouses' are called mice."

Mr Hodges enquired whether the boy had a proper cage at home for the new family. With pride, Casey gave the vet a vivid description of a large cage he'd been given, along with feeding bottles, food trays and exercise wheels. Mr Hodges told him that he would need to see the mice at a later stage, to sort out the boys from the girls. But to prevent the boy from attempting to carry the little creatures to the clinic once again, Emma volunteered to visit Casey at his home and do the job. She also had two spare cages Casey would need to keep the sexes apart – if he didn't want to be over-run with mice.

"Thanks, Mr Hodges," said the small boy, pulling a grubby polythene bag full of five-pence pieces from his pocket and handing them to the vet.

"No, Casey. Certainly no charge for congratulations to a mum and her five healthy babies," the kindly man replied.

"See you soon," promised Emma, showing him out. "Hold that box tightly, Casey." She took a slim booklet about keeping mice, gerbils and hamsters from a display stand on the reception desk and slipped it into Casey's pocket. The boy beamed his gratitude.

The small veterinary practice in Handley Road was popular with the local residents — and even more so since Emma had been assisting her father. The children, especially, liked to spend time with her. There was also no doubting the effect she had on most of the animals who walked, or were carried, through the clinic doors. They seemed to sense a calmness about her born out of a genuine love and interest in them. On occasions, Emma sat in the waiting room comforting a nervous animal before it went into the surgery. Mr Hodges had been particularly impressed when his daughter had led Henry, an exceptionally nervous Spaniel, into his room one morning. Usually, the poor dog had to be lifted, as rigid as a statue, and placed on the examination table. There, he would continue to quake before subsiding on to his haunches. To the surprise of Mr Hodges and Henry's owner, the dog had obediently accompanied Emma into the surgery, where he'd stood quite firmly on four legs throughout his examination. This had been the result of Emma spending some time with him in the waiting room beforehand. Stroking and comforting him, she had let him gain a sense of trust in her before she'd led him, as docile as a lamb, through the doors. Once inside she had stayed with him throughout his examination. Emma believed that any animal, possibly whisked from a warm and comfortable basket at home into a place filled with unfamiliar odours and other animals, would be more than a little apprehensive.

Emma loved nothing better than the chance to be around animals. Her brother, Jack, was already on the road to becoming a vet. He was twenty and attending veterinary college. It meant living away from home and years of hard work and study, if he was to qualify. Mr Hodges had hoped Jack's future lay in working alongside him in the practice, but his son had other ideas. The big animals found on farms were of more interest to Jack, and working alongside livestock, rather than his dad, was where he envisaged his career to be. Mr Hodges had been disappointed at first, although he had received some very clear signals that another member of his family was very keen to work with him – if she was given half a chance.

Emma leaned across the reception desk and took a card with details of the next patient. Seeing it was a dog reminded her again of Buster. The sullen-looking boy hadn't shown up with him. Perhaps her handiwork had been sufficient, after all, and the dog's paw was fine. Even so, Emma wished he could be checked over by her father. Sue the receptionist looked up and ran her fingers through a thick cluster of auburn curls; yet again they had escaped the hairpins fighting to keep them under control. She smiled at Emma and whispered, "Good luck with Mrs Higgins and Walter, Em. I've been round the waiting room with the air-freshener twice, since they arrived, but it hasn't defeated that horrible pong." Sue wrinkled her little freckled nose, pinching the end of it to demonstrate her dislike of the unpleasant smell filling the room. Emma tried not to giggle, noticing at the same time that the good-natured receptionist was right: there was more than a nasty whiff in the air. And, it was definitely coming from the direction of glum-looking Mrs Higgins and Walter her Pekinese.

As she bent to stroke Walter's frail-looking form, Emma looked into the dog's huge, watery eyes. They were black and the size of marbles. Seeing him nestled in his owner's lap, his soft hair fluffed out around him, Emma was reminded of a broody chicken. "Would you like to bring Walter through, now, Mrs Higgins?" she invited.

The thin elderly lady wore an expression every bit as miserable and anxious as that of her dog. She clutched Walter to her chest and followed Emma into her father's surgery. Before Mrs Higgins had even commented on Walter's condition, Mr Hodges had become

16

aware of the strange, unpleasant odour wafting into his room. Reaching to open the top window, he turned to smile at the lady.

"Poor Walter, Mr Hodges. He's come out all over in a horrible rash. I'm beside myself with worry. I don't know what to do for him. Keeps scratching himself."

Mr Hodges reached out to help place the dog on the table. The pathetic creature left Mrs Higgins' arms with reluctance. Calm and confident, the vet made a brief examination of the dog, whose enormous eyes swivelled sideways to look pitifully up at his distressed owner.

"There, there, Walter," cooed Mrs Higgins. "Mr Hodges just wants to have a look at you."

Emma watched her father as he gently moved aside the long fronds of pale, golden hair to reveal the dog's skin beneath its coat. There, an angry red rash had formed in patches over its back and sides.

"I bet he checks the dog's eyes next," thought Emma. She had guessed correctly. Very carefully, Mr Hodges cradled Walter's head in one hand while he peered closely into the dog's eyes. Then, he felt along the animal's quarters. He stood back, considering his patient for a moment, before speaking.

"Some sort of allergic reaction has caused these sore patches on Walter. Can you think of anything out of the ordinary with which he may have been in contact recently?"

Mrs Higgins frowned as she considered the question, before shaking her head and replying she knew of nothing that could be responsible.

"I can't help but notice the strange smell Walter has about him," commented Mr Hodges, politely moving in for a quick sniff. So far he had been unable to identify the smell. "Fortunately the skin is unbroken, but if he continues to scratch I'm afraid he soon will go through – and that could prove to be very sore."

Emma, who had been deep in thought, suddenly ventured: "I've been trying to work out just what it is about the smell that seems sort of familiar. It's like scent that's gone off. Yes! *That's it!* – like mouldy aftershave."

Mrs Higgins suddenly turned very pale and looked uncomfortable. She muttered, "It *is* aftershave. I had to spray *something* on Walter's fur to cover up the awful smell of my husband's old pipe tobacco. I've told him before: Walter and I don't like the stink. It stays on my clothes and in Walter's lovely coat for days."

Before she had finished speaking a look of horror came into her eyes. Then they filled with tears. Mr Hodges appeared concerned, and Emma moved to the distressed lady's side to put an arm around her shoulder.

"It's *my* fault, isn't it, Mr Hodges? *I've* done this to my poor Walter. I've sprayed him and caused his awful rash. However will I be able to live with myself?"

"Don't worry, Mrs Higgins," said Mr Hodges, trying to reassure her. "It'll clear up. It's more than likely that old aftershave has caused his skin to react; animals' skin is different from ours. But I'm sure Walter will soon be fine again."

Emma handed Mrs Higgins a tissue. Cautiously, the elderly lady began to stroke her dog's head. The big watery eyes stared up at her. They seemed full of affection. Mr Hodges placed Walter in Mrs Higgins' arms and said, "I'll write out a prescription for some antiseptic cream and some solution you can use to bathe Walter. Apply the cream very sparingly. If you have any trouble, we'll do it for you. And Mrs Higgins, please don't worry. Sue will make an appointment for you to bring him back in about a week."

As Emma showed the lady and her beloved pet out of the surgery, she felt secretly pleased with herself for acting on a notion. Her nostrils had solved the mystery of Walter's rash. She returned to her father with a broad beam of self-satisfaction on her face, but when she looked into his face, he wasn't smiling. Mr Hodges was far from pleased.

# Chapter 3

"I know you guessed right, Emma, and your intuition paid off. Poor old Walter had been doused in something pretty strong and foul-smelling. But *please*, next time you have a brainwave, talk to me first. Just take me quietly to one side and say we need to discuss something. Mrs Higgins is old and frail, and Walter is such an important part of her life. Even though it was unintentional, it must have been awful for her to realize that *she* had caused him any kind of discomfort. We must remember that although we're here to treat the animals, their owners also need care and consideration."

Emma stared at the floor. She felt dreadful: her father was right. Angry with herself, she faced him and apologized. "I'm *really* sorry. I just acted on an impulse. It was as though the smell suddenly rang bells with me. Nan hangs on to old scent for years, so I realized I'd smelled something like it before."

The tall man smiled down at his daughter, recollecting how keen he'd been at vet college to come up with the right answers.

Emma took a deep breath, stood up straight and asked, "Shall I show in the next patient, Dad?"

"Please," returned her father, satisfied with her apology and her readiness to get back to work.

When Emma walked out into the waiting room, Mrs Higgins was just going out through the door, smothering Walter with kisses. A quick glance told Emma that some new patients had arrived. A young girl with her mother sat balancing a cage containing a lively brown hamster. It was skilfully swinging, Tarzan-like, from bar to bar along the top of its cage. Emma wondered whether, like the last two hamsters brought in, this one was also named Hammy.

She was just about to take another card with details of the next patient, when Sue the receptionist spoke to her.

"If you're making a cup of tea, Em, I wouldn't say no." Sue let her head flop down on to the pile of files she was sorting through, and let her tongue hang out of her mouth, pretending she was desperate for liquid. Emma smiled, picked up the card and showed the next patient into her father's surgery. Then she went off to make some tea.

Emma had liked Sue from the very first moment she'd arrived to take up the job of receptionist at her father's practice. She was big and cuddly; warm-hearted and a lot of fun. It had been the fact that she was friendly and loved animals that had persuaded Mr Hodges to employ her. He had overlooked her disorganized methods, infuriating as they could be at times. He considered her ability to swing into action in the event of an emergency, to be far more important.

Sue lived alone apart from the company of

her dog: an aging cross-breed "something", as she referred to Victor, or Old Vic, as he was better known. He was large, mostly black, with a few grey patches, and very affectionate when awake. Sue brought him to work every day and, although he had the freedom of the little garden at the practice, he preferred to snooze the hours away in an old armchair behind the reception desk.

Emma stirred two sugars into her father's tea and placed Sue's huge mug, decorated with cats, next to it on a tray which she then carried through to reception.

# Chapter 4

Emma waved a chocolate biscuit under Sue's nose and teased, "Are you sure about sticking with that boring old diet?"

"Oh, give it *here*. I'll go back on the cottage cheese and watercress tomorrow," Sue replied, eagerly grabbing the biscuit and taking a huge bite.

The telephone rang, and as Sue's mouth was crammed with chocolate digestive, Emma put down the tray with her father's rapidly cooling tea and spoke into the receiver:

"Good morning. Handley Road Veterinary Clinic. Can I help you?" she enquired in a bright, efficient voice. A look of confusion spread over her features as the voice on the other end made an enquiry. Then she answered, "I'm sorry, but did I hear you say you've got a sick Boa Constrictor? Only I'm afraid a large reptile like that will need specialist attention. This is a small veterinary practice, but if you hold on, I can get some numbers for you to contact."

There was silence at the other end of the line before a young man's voice chuckled, "That won't be necessary – I think he's got a grip of himself again!"

Emma exploded: "*Jack!* You're *horrid*! You actually fooled me this time." Then she began to giggle. "Get off the line. Dad would be annoyed if he knew you were calling reception, unless it's urgent – which it obviously is *not*."

Jack, Emma's older brother, who was in veterinary college in the middle of the country, was in the habit of trying to catch his sister out whenever he telephoned. She usually recognized him, but this time, while her thoughts had returned again to wonder about the fate of Buster, he'd managed to catch her off guard. She realized that when he next came home she would be in for some merciless teasing. Emma laughed along with him.

"Well, what do you want, and when are you coming home again?" she demanded. Emma was delighted when her red-haired six-foot brother, with his scruffy clothes and permanently out-of-tune guitar, came to stay. There was always lots of laughter when Jack was in the house, as well as untidy heaps of clothing everywhere. Her face broke into a broad smile. "Next Saturday – great! Mum had better start stocking up on food for you." Emma could hear her father moving towards his surgery door, so she hurriedly finished the call with her brother.

Mr Hodges was showing out a boy with his guinea-pig. Emma glanced at the mug of tea on the tray, noticing a thin, cold film had formed over its surface. She would need to make him a fresh one.

"I won't be a moment, Dad. I've just heard some good news. Next Saturday, Jack's driving down to spend a few weeks with us."

Mr Hodges looked delighted at the news.

He enjoyed the long discussions, sometimes arguments, he had about work with his son. His thoughts returned to his work. There were a lot more animals and their owners to be seen before Jack was due home.

# Chapter 5

"You've only got one more patient, Dad," announced Emma towards the end of morning surgery "I'll help Sue tidy up in reception, then put the CLOSED sign up for the day." Emma began to busy herself in the waiting room, picking up tufts of stray dog hair and making two neat piles of the magazines left lying around.

Sue stood up, stretched and sighed: "Can't wait to get my feet up, Em. There's a good weepy film on later. I'll cuddle up with Old Vic on the sofa and have a good cry. Won't we?" she said to the aging dog as she popped a couple of Doggy Choc-drops into his mouth.

Emma was just about to approach the door, to turn the sign from OPEN to CLOSED, when she was startled by the sudden appearance of a tall figure framed in the doorway. It was the boy she had met the day before and, cradled in his arms, was Buster.

"You were right," he muttered when Emma opened the door. "I should have brought him before. He's not at all well."

Sue emerged from behind her desk, concerned to see the late arrivals.

"It's all right, Sue." She beckoned him in. "I asked him to fetch the dog in." Then turning to the boy, Emma said, "We're just about to close but I'm sure my dad will see you."

The boy was obviously uncomfortable. "Look, you might as well know – I've got no money at the moment to pay for any treatment."

Emma sensed his embarrassment and told him not to worry. She would explain to her father. When Mr Hodges opened his surgery door, Emma took him to one side and quietly told him about Buster, explaining the incident the previous afternoon. Mr Hodges was concerned that his daughter had waded into a group of boys to treat an unfamiliar dog in the street. However docile the dog appeared, it could have turned on her when she'd attempted to remove the splinter. Mr Hodges beckoned the boy and his dog into the surgery. Once Buster was on the examination table, the vet carefully unbound the handkerchief from the injured paw. Pus oozed from the wound. Emma was pleased to notice that the boy immediately leaned forward and very gently stroked Buster's head.

"Well, whoever removed the splinter," announced Mr Hodges, giving his daughter a wry smile, "made a nice clean job of it. But I'm glad you brought him to see me," he added, looking at the boy. "That paw is beginning to turn nasty. I'll need to give him an injection of antibiotics to get the infection on the move. We'll put a clean dressing on the wound too. Try not to let him run around on it for a few days, and keep the dressing dry. I'd like to see him again next Saturday."

Buster accepted his injection well and sat

perfectly still while his paw was bathed, cleaned out and dressed. He seemed to recognize Emma, his soft, brown eyes often turning to focus on her.

The boy shuffled uneasily from the surgery with Buster in his arms when it was time for him to leave. At the entrance he turned to Emma and spoke quietly: "Thanks. I'm really grateful for what your dad's done for Buster – and for your help, too. Like I said, I've got no money now, but I'll pay as soon as I can. I've been unemployed since I left school – just can't get work with the hours I need." He broke off abruptly, began to walk away, then suddenly turned. The flicker of a smile moved across his face. "By the way," he added, "I'm called Jamie – and my mates aren't as bad as you might think. They were really impressed by the way you handled Buster yesterday."

# Chapter 6

"Emma – *please* have just a nibble of breakfast before you go downstairs to help your dad," implored Jane Hodges, Emma's mother.

"Sorry, Mum – haven't the time. I'm late as it is."

Saturday morning had found Emma as keen as ever to work alongside her father. A week had passed since she had seen Buster and his owner Jamie. She was anticipating a return visit from them, hoping to see a big improvement in the dog's paw.

Emma had finished her homework late the previous night and as a result had overslept. When it came to her morning in the surgery, feeding herself came low on her list of priorities. She loved being around the place: listening, observing, and helping whenever she could be of use. Even if one of the veterinary nurses was performing the simplest procedure, Emma was only too pleased for the opportunity to watch every detail. All the first-hand experience would serve her well when she entered veterinary college; and she was determined about that.

Emma showed Mrs Higgins and her beloved dog Walter into her father's surgery for their return visit. Mr Hodges was pleased with the improvement in the dog's skin. The angry red blotches were definitely on the move, fading to little more than pale pink patches, which Walter no longer found it necessary to scratch. As Mr Hodges stroked the timid dog's head, he reassured Mrs Higgins that Walter was looking so much better. She beamed with pleasure at his remark, delighting in telling the vet how brave her dog had been while she applied the cream or bathed him.

Emma could hear the tinkle of the little

bell above the entrance as the waiting room began to fill with people and their animals. It was going to be a busy morning. As Mr Hodges lifted Walter from the examination table back into the eager arms of his owner, he paused for a moment. A woman's shrieks had suddenly filled the air, causing Mrs Higgins to jump and almost drop Walter. The piercing sounds were coming from the waiting room. Within seconds, Sue the receptionist called out to the vet: "It's all right, Mr Hodges. No real need for alarm. Casey has just arrived with some new creatures – but don't worry, we'll soon find them again."

Sue's last remark did little to put Mr Hodges at ease when he attempted to reassure Mrs Higgins that all was well. Standing, clutching Walter to her chest, the poor woman had begun to wonder whether every visit to the vet was going to cause her palpitations. Emma required only one quick glance from her father, to understand that he wanted her to investigate the disturbance in the waiting room.

\*　\*　\*

"It's *slow-worms* this time, Em," announced Sue indicating Casey, who was scrambling about on hands and knees beneath the chair of a terrified woman who'd brought her cat in. "I told Casey not to take them out of the box, but the minute I was on the phone, he opened it."

The distraught woman, squatting on a chair with her knees drawn up close to her chest, squealed: "*Horrible*, slimy little snakes! They were crawling all over my lap. *Please* hurry up and catch them!"

Emma dropped to her knees beside Casey. The young boy looked very ill-at-ease as he whispered, "I'm sorry. I just told that lady's son what was in my box, and he asked me for a look. All I did was pick one of them up, but when his mum saw it she screamed and I dropped the box. It sort of fell in her lap." Casey's expression suddenly changed and he looked indignant as he reflected on the lady's words. "They're not slimy little snakes! I brought them along to show your dad — thought he might be interested."

Emma frowned. "I'm not sure that Dad

will be wildly enthusiastic about seeing them during a busy Saturday morning surgery, especially if they're scaring the wits out of his clients. Come on, let's get them back in the box as quickly as possible."

Just as Emma finished speaking, one of the slim delicately-featured creatures appeared from behind a chair. In an instant, Casey lunged. In one swift move he secured the slow-worm in his hands and popped it smartly back in the box. The frightened woman shuddered as she caught a brief glimpse of it before covering her eyes. But Casey's sudden arrest of the creature hadn't gone unnoticed by two small dogs. They sensed the other slow-worm was still on the loose at ground level, and it was definitely spooking them. In unison, they began to bark, which in turn caused Old Vic to object to his disturbed snooze with a lazy, gruff woof. Bewildered mews from inside the cat basket soon added to the chorus.

"Oh *Casey*!" exclaimed Emma in an exasperated voice.

Casey continued to grovel about on the

floor, until the door to Mr Hodges' room opened very slowly. It revealed the tall figure of the vet. Cowering behind him was Mrs Higgins, looking bewildered. Both were just in time to see Emma perform a less than elegant dive between an elderly man with a squawking budgie, and the lady with the cat. In an instant, Emma had caught the other slow-worm as it started to slither across the floor.

A cup of tea and some reassuring words from Sue had finally managed to calm the woman frightened by Casey's latest acquisition. Mr Hodges had some words of warning for the young boy. He told him that he appreciated his enthusiasm where animals were concerned, but cautioned him about adding to the mini-zoo he already owned. He felt Casey had more than enough creatures to care for. Casey slipped out with the box secured beneath his arm, as silent as a slow-worm.

It had been a very busy morning, even more so due to Casey's episode. Emma had still found opportunities to check whether her brother Jack had come home, but mostly to see if Jamie and Buster had arrived. Now, the morning surgery was almost over. There had been no sign of them.

"A penny for your thoughts, Em?" quizzed Sue as she showed the last patient out and turned the OPEN sign on the door to CLOSED.

Emma, who had been gazing vacantly into space while wondering about the boy and his dog, replied, "I'm disappointed that Buster and Jamie didn't turn up."

Sue looked thoughtful. "Strange boy," she mused. "It's as though he's got something to hide. I don't mean there's anything sinister about him, but he's just – well – sort of secretive."

Emma smiled to herself, remembering how Sue often made observations which proved to have more than a grain of truth in them.

"He mentioned something about not being able to get a job with the right hours," commented Emma. "He seemed reluctant to say any more. Makes you wonder what he meant though."

# Chapter 7

Emma woke with a start in the early hours of the morning. She could feel her heart pounding. There was someone moving about at the bottom of the stairs outside her door. A creak on the first one told her that someone was actually climbing them. Emma often managed to remain calm in the face of a crisis, but waking to discover an intruder only a matter of steps away produced muddled thinking on this occasion. Should she make a dash for it and rush to her parents' room, or stay put and huddle down on the other side of the bed, hoping that whoever it was would just go away?

For a moment, she considered alerting her

parents by tapping gently on the adjoining wall. Or had they already heard the intruder? Before Emma could decide the best course of action, Rosie, the family's labrador, who slept at the end of her bed, sat bolt upright and inclined an ear towards the door. There was another squeak on the stairs as the unwanted night-visitor moved nearer. The dog growled and bared her teeth. Then, all was still – the person on the other side couldn't have failed to hear Rosie. Emma decided there was nothing else for it but to let the dog loose.

As she moved swiftly to the door and crouched down ready to turn the handle, she fancied she could hear panting close by. Another creak from a stair tread informed her that the intruder had made it to the top step. To Emma's surprise Rosie, who was lying low, her nose sniffing along the base of the door, suddenly started to wag her tail. Emma interpreted the gesture as the dog's eagerness to deal with the night prowler. Restraining her for a moment, with a firm grip on her collar, Emma quickly turned the doorknob and swung wide the door. With loud barks, Rosie raced from the room into the dark of the landing.

"*Go girl!*" shrieked Emma. For a second, a tall figure in the shadows stood perched on the top step, frozen like a statue. Then, under Rosie's excited attack and uttering the words: "It's *meeeeee!*" the figure tumbled backwards from the top step. In a series of thuds and anguished cries, it hit every step as it bumped its way to the bottom of the staircase. There, it lay still and crumpled like an old discarded coat.

When Mr Hodges switched on the landing light, it revealed a pitiful scene below. Emma clasped her hand to her mouth, shocked at the sight. Among the scattered contents of a rucksack and the shattered remains of his old guitar, her brother Jack lay motionless. No sound came from his lips. The only noise was that of Rosie eagerly licking his face while she wagged her tail, delighted to be reunited with an old friend.

Mrs Hodges, who had followed her husband at the sound of the commotion, rushed downstairs with him to crouch over their son. The vet felt for Jack's pulse. As he touched him, the crumpled form suddenly opened its eyes and spoke.

"Oh *no*, Dad! I've landed on my guitar and crushed it."

Mrs Hodges sobbed with relief. "Trust Jack to worry about that dreadful instrument at a time like this." Much to Mr Hodges' relief, it appeared that Jack hadn't come to much harm, other than some stiff limbs, a few bruises and the temporary shock of the fall. Emma crept guiltily down the stairs to her brother.

"I'm sorry about letting Rosie loose on you, Jack." The discomfort in her voice sounded obvious. "I thought you were a burglar. I had to do *something*. Anyway, what on *earth* were you doing creeping around the house at this time of the morning? You said you'd be home on Saturday. Why didn't you phone?"

Before Jack had a chance to reply, Mr Hodges had challenged his daughter. "And, what were *you* doing, trying to take on an intruder single-handed? It might well have been a burglar." Emma was saved from having to explain her impetuous actions when Jack produced a series of grunts and groans as he attempted to sit up. With a pained expression on his face he related how his old car had broken down on the motorway. The last thing he'd expected to encounter on arriving home in the early hours of the morning was an over-enthusiastic welcome from the family dog. He hadn't wanted to wake anyone and thought he'd just creep upstairs to bed.

Jack reached for the wrecked guitar. Broken strings stuck out in all directions. He held it limply in his hands; his expression was sad. Everyone said how sorry they were to see his beloved instrument, obviously beyond repair. Secretly, each one of them was relieved. They would be spared Jack's tuneless strummings until he got his hands on another one.

By mid-morning all members of the family were awake, though tired from the earlier events. Everyone, that is, except Jack. He slept peacefully throughout the morning.

Emma had looked in on him before going down to breakfast. She reflected that it was incredible he hadn't been seriously hurt. Sunday was unusually quiet considering Jack was home. Emma found her thoughts straying to Buster once again.

# Chapter 8

"Don't spoil Jack too much, Mum," was Emma's passing remark as she left for school on Monday morning. "You know he'll make the most of his tumble and have you running all over the place."

Taking her usual well-worn route to school, Emma began to wonder how Buster was faring, and why Jamie hadn't brought him back for her father to check him over. She walked past a turning lined on either side with tiny old terraced houses. Most of them were in need of repair. Unknowingly, Emma had passed within a short distance of Buster's home.

\* \* \*

In a kitchen, gloomy and cramped but very clean and tidy, Buster snoozed the hours away next to Jamie's gran. His paw was healing well and he was comfortable. The stone floor in the little room was covered with worn-out mats which had been shaken and swept by Jamie that morning. He had washed all the breakfast things and stacked them to dry before going out. Jamie's gran stared up at the old clock noisily marking the passing of the day. The stout, elderly lady reached out to re-arrange a blanket covering her legs, the joints swollen and painful with arthritis. Jamie was very fond of his gran. She was a sweet lady who seldom complained about her condition, and the difficulty of moving about in a tiny house with a walking-frame. Only when Jamie was able to push her in a wheelchair was she ever able to go out for any length of time.

When Jamie had arrived home one afternoon with Buster, his gran had been delighted at the prospect of having the timid mongrel with the big, soft brown eyes for company. Buster had been very nervous at

47

first, shying away whenever she'd reached to stroke his head. The animal shelter where Jamie had obtained him said Buster hadn't been particularly well treated by his previous owner. There were signs of poor nourishment, infrequent exercise and general neglect. Jamie was told to be prepared for the dog to take time in building up trust. A quiet existence at home with his gran would be a good start. But that didn't mean Buster need lead a secluded life. It was important for him to have plenty of walks and become used to the streets and parks in the locality.

Buster had soon settled in and formed an attachment for the old lady, who often saved him tasty little scraps from her plate as a treat. He always appeared eager to accompany Jamie when he took him out. As the months passed he learned to trust Jamie as both his master and friend. When he had time, Jamie tried to teach the dog some simple commands, but it didn't prove to be an easy task; Buster had never been trained as a puppy.

The ticking of the clock was interrupted

by a sudden loud knocking at the front door. Jamie's gran chose to ignore it. She wasn't expecting anyone. But when it was repeated she wondered whether it might be Jamie; perhaps he had forgotten his key. The instant she struggled to her feet, Buster was up too, tail wagging and anxious to follow her. It took the old lady some time to manoeuvre her walking-frame along the narrow hallway to the door. Exhausted and out of breath, she eventually managed to open it to the persistent caller. An eager young salesman stood in front of her. Oozing confidence he thrust a handful of brochures, featuring home-improvement schemes, in front of her and launched into his sales routine. Leaning on her walking-frame, Jamie's gran struggled to retain her balance, but it was difficult with the door wedged open. She wished her grandson was home to deter the man; he didn't seem to be hearing her when she told him she wasn't interested. After what seemed like a very long time to the old lady, the young salesman decided that he'd spent enough energy trying to convince her of his.

incredible offers. It was time to move on to another house. Buster, who had followed her to the door, poked his head out during the ordeal and sniffed, drawing the odours from the street deep into his nostrils. To him they smelled exciting – enticing.

Jamie's gran was so busy adjusting the position of her walking frame that she didn't notice Buster slipping out as she struggled to close the door.

# Chapter 9

The dry, dusty pavements felt good beneath Buster's paws, despite one of them still being dressed with the bandage Mr Hodges had applied. The antibiotics had soon taken effect. Buster felt fine as he padded along the road, pausing to sniff at an interesting scent on a lamppost or to lick water from a near-dry puddle.

Buster's excursion took him to places he hadn't visited before: places a dog on the loose would find well worth investigating. As he strolled along back alleys, littered with rubbish and tall weeds, he was surprised when he came face to face with other animals. Turning down a damp, foul-smelling, narrow alleyway, he was suddenly confronted by a large, panting bundle of matted dog hair, wobbling on ancient legs. The old dog had been sniffing at a rotting box which had once contained a burger. At Buster's approach the dog's heavy, dusty head looked up and opened its mouth to reveal a few broken, yellowing teeth. A throaty bark served as warning: the rotting box belonged to him – and Buster was on *his* territory. Buster backed off close to the wall. Although he sensed the old dog posed no real danger, and even with an injured paw he could out-run him, he decided to move away and leave the creature jealously guarding his possession.

Before Buster had made it to the other end of the alleyway he found himself in the presence of a far more dangerous challenge. A spindly-legged ginger cat leapt from one of the walls and, back arched, blocked Buster's path. The dog froze when the cat suddenly spat at him. Then, without warning, it lashed out with a powerful swipe, unsheathing barbed claws from a front paw. The blow caught Buster across his nose and he yelped, reeling backwards, only just dodging a second well-aimed attack. Dashing from the alleyway into the open once more, he let the fresher air rush in and fill his lungs. A quick look back at the cat, still poised for combat, and the old dog rummaging further up the alley, encouraged him to move on.

## Chapter 10

"Feels as though it was only a few hours ago that I was walking *to* school," thought Emma on her way home later that day. "Now, the same old plod home again. And at the end of it –" she sighed deeply – "physics, German, and some *boring* old map of somewhere thousands of miles away that I'm never likely to visit." She quickly dismissed the thought and comforted herself with visions of a kitten recently brought into the clinic. As soon as tea was over, she intended to cuddle the fluffy little creature.

Emma stood at the side of the road waiting to cross the busy street. The smell of petrol fumes from the cars and dust on the road made her sneeze several times in succession. Between a brief gap in the traffic, she was able to see across to the other side. What she saw disturbed her. Walking aimlessly along the pavement, trailing a grubby dressing from his paw, was Buster. Emma was both concerned and angry. How *could* Jamie allow his dog to wander the streets unaccompanied? She puzzled for a moment as to what she should do next. Soon resolving there was little she could do until it was possible to cross to the island in the middle of the road, Emma just hoped Buster would stay put. But the loud, abrupt honking of an impatient driver on Emma's side of the road, made Buster turn and look in her direction. He seemed to recognize her and plodded towards the edge of the kerb. When he became certain it was her, he began to wag his tail and bark with approval. A cold shiver ran the length of Emma's spine; the traffic was heavy and fast, and Buster looked poised for action.

"*Please stay*," she whispered between clenched teeth as her pulse began to race. But

Buster was teetering on the very edge of the pavement, one front paw held above the kerb. He looked at her again and barked another friendly greeting.

Emma noticed that a man now stood next to Buster, waiting to cross. He seemed oblivious to the lone dog so close to the fast-moving traffic. When the man glanced in Emma's direction, she tried to attract his attention by waving at him and pointing to Buster. He appeared confused, peering hard at her, wondering if they were acquainted. "Look at the *dog*," Emma mouthed to him, indicating Buster. The man, who still appeared to be in some confusion, and a little embarrassed, just frowned and looked away. He thought Emma was behaving very strangely. Buster, however, had become excited by seeing Emma waving and took a step forward into the road. Emma's hand went to her mouth: "*No, stay!*" she screamed. For a moment he froze and, with head tilted on one side, looked straight at her as the procession of vehicles continued to pass. To her relief he suddenly took a step back again.

Emma breathed out a great sigh. Glancing both ways along the road, she noticed a gap would soon be appearing in the traffic, and she should be able to cross to the little island. Once there, a repeated STAY command to Buster might just keep him still until she was able to reach his side in safety. The dog's tail had started to wag again in anticipation of meeting her.

"Just two more cars," thought Emma, preparing to move. But the impatient dog couldn't wait another second. In one bound Buster was in the road and dashing towards Emma – straight into the path of an oncoming van. Emma squeezed her eyes tight shut, unable to watch the inevitable collision as the van hit Buster. He was tossed into the air, then with an audible thud, fell motionless to the ground. Sounds and smells flooded Emma's ears and nostrils: the sickening screech of brakes; the smell of burning rubber from tyres skidding to a halt; and everywhere, the reek of petrol fumes.

On unsteady legs Emma moved like a robot into the road where Buster lay. The owner of the van that had hit him was shaken but fortunately unhurt. He stood alongside Emma.

"Just dashed into the road right in front of me, he did. There was *no* way I could have avoided him." He repeated himself several times, telling others as they began to gather at the scene. Soon a little island of people had formed around Buster and Emma, who had bent to crouch over him. All the traffic had come to a halt too. Further back, some drivers honked their annoyance at being delayed, obviously unaware of the accident that lay ahead of them.

With sadness, Emma viewed the pathetic sight of the mongrel who had recently been so pleased to see her. Taking a closer look, she noticed a thin trickle of blood forming at the corner of Buster's mouth. He looked lifeless, but still she bent over his body and listened to his chest, watching for signs of breathing. The rise and fall of his chest seemed barely visible to her. Somebody called for the crowd to move away to allow Emma more room. She stood up, realizing there was nothing more she could do apart from ask a man to fetch her father from his clinic, while she remained with Buster.

Two men took it upon themselves to help direct the traffic around the van. The impatient drivers who had honked and revved their engines now fell silent as they filed past and stared at the girl and the dog by the roadside. Emma kept focused on the rise and fall of Buster's chest. She asked the van driver if he had an old blanket or anything similar she could put over Buster to keep him warm. The man willingly rummaged around in the back of his van and produced a ragged jacket which Emma carefully lay over the dog.

It seemed only a matter of minutes before Mr Hodges arrived with a small stretcher, and Jack close on his heels. As Mr Hodges crouched down next to Buster, preparing to make a brief examination, the dog suddenly opened its eyes. Lifting his head with a dazed expression, Buster struggled to stand on shaking legs, but immediately collapsed with a yelp to the ground. "It's shock, Jack. At first, I thought he was unconscious. Let's get him to the clinic and see what we can find."

Buster put up little resistance as Jack and Mr Hodges manoeuvred him on to the stretcher; he just lay licking his lips. They tried not to jolt him as they moved swiftly along the road. Emma placed one hand on Buster to keep him steady. As they approached the entrance, she turned at the sound of loud footsteps. Someone was running towards them. Jamie came to a sudden halt at Buster's side. Emma anticipated his first question and, before he had a chance to catch his breath to ask it, she confirmed: "Yes. He's alive."

Jamie knelt down and cradled Buster's head gently in his arms.

But Mr Hodges insisted: "Let's get him in. I need to get a saline drip up."

Within moments Buster was rushed into the operating room. The door was shut with a resounding finality that made Emma shiver. Everything had happened so quickly. She had a lot of faith in her father's ability, but was also aware that road accidents could cause severe internal injuries. Despite the impact of the van on Buster, he didn't appear to have dreadful external injuries. But it was that little trickle of blood at the side of his mouth that concerned Emma. Was it a sign that all was far from well internally? Could there be haemorrhaging? The sights and sounds of the accident came back to her and she tried to shut them out by concentrating on comforting Jamie.

# Chapter 11

Jamie had stared into space with a blank expression on his face for what seemed like ages. Mr Hodges and Jack had been with Buster for a long time. Emma had tried to speak to Jamie but he was reluctant to talk. She wanted to ask him why Buster had been roaming the streets alone, but knew it was obviously the wrong moment. Suddenly Jamie stood up and turned his long, thin features towards her.

"I've got to go," he announced, looking even more anxious. A finger went to his mouth and he chewed on an already well-bitten fingernail. "Look," he said, staring hard into Emma's face, as though he were about to make a confession. "I must go and cook a meal for my gran. She suffers badly with arthritis. It's difficult for her to care for herself – there's no one else, you see. I get her meals, give her the medicine she needs and put her to bed – that sort of thing." He looked away, embarrassed. "If I couldn't do it, she'd have to go into a home." With a sad note in his voice, he continued: "I never want that to happen." Jamie pushed his lank hair off his face and added: "And now Gran's blaming herself for Buster's accident, because he slipped out of the front door when she opened it to a salesman. I dashed out to look for Buster the moment I got home and Gran told me he'd gone." Now he sounded angry. "*None* of this would have happened if I hadn't been out looking for work again."

As Emma sat listening to the boy she was filled with pity. So that's what he'd been so secretive about. On the outside he looked just like his tough mates on the street, but in reality his life was centred around caring for his gran. Emma supposed he felt that bit didn't fit in with the image he wanted others to see. She would have liked to tell him what a good character she thought he had; not many boys of his age would dedicate their time to an old lady's needs. But Emma felt sure any comments like that would only cause him further embarrassment. Instead, she simply asked him to leave his telephone number. She would explain the situation to her dad, and as soon as there was news of Buster's condition, they would be in contact with him. Jamie hurriedly scribbled his number and handed it to Emma.

"You mustn't blame yourself, Jamie. You and your gran didn't intentionally let Buster loose. Go home and reassure her that it certainly wasn't her fault Buster was injured. I only wish *I* had been able to prevent him from dashing into the road."

Jamie shuffled out of the door and Emma busied herself around the waiting room. It helped to pass the time until her father and Jack came out. Eventually they emerged. Emma was eager to hear all they had to say.

"It seems incredible. We've x-rayed, but

nothing, at present, appears to be badly damaged, although he's suffered a lot of bruising. It's definitely his hind area that's taken the impact, and this sort of accident often results in damage to hips or a broken femur. Buster has a slight fracture to one of his hindlegs, which we've plastered. Now we need to watch him overnight, and for a few days, to make sure we've not overlooked anything, and his condition remains stable." Emma explained to her father why Jamie had left. Mr Hodges took his number and went to phone over news of Buster's condition.

Emma entered the operating room and saw Buster for the first time since the accident. She was used to seeing animals who'd been injured on the road, but because it was Buster, and she had witnessed the incident, it seemed to affect her all the more. The poor dog was laid out on the table, his freshly plastered hindleg uppermost. He looked very weak, but when Emma leaned over him, he showed a flicker of recognition in his big brown eyes. She knew he must be feeling afraid and very uncomfortable.

"Poor Buster," she whispered, "you seemed so pleased to see me in the street. If only I could have prevented that awful accident in some way."

Tyres screeched to a standstill at the traffic lights not far below Emma's bedroom window. She opened her eyes and slipped out of bed to pull back the curtain. Only when she saw a gleaming convertible car roar away, the moment the lights changed, was she satisfied that she wasn't part of a terrible nightmare, replaying Buster's accident. Emma had found it hard to get to sleep that night. She'd lain awake worrying about Buster. He had come through a horrible accident, which she was amazed he had survived. Still deliberating over whether she could, in some way, have prevented it, she eventually dozed off.

Emma yawned and, pulling on her dressing-gown, walked downstairs to see whether it was her brother or father sitting up with Buster. Jack looked up as she entered the room. He had been listening to Buster's heart.

Buster lay in the same position as Emma had last seen him, before going to bed. She ran a finger over one of his soft, floppy ears. Her brother rubbed his eyes, yawned several times and sank down on to a stool.

"Let me sit with him while you get some sleep, Jack," Emma volunteered. "I'm really not very tired and I could call you or Dad if there's any sudden change."

Jack considered, then looked relieved. "Well, I certainly could do with getting my head down for a couple of hours. Thanks, but fetch one of us if anything unusual happens."

Emma watched her brother run his hand through his thick mop of red hair as he walked out of the door. She pulled up a stool and sat close to Buster. Her imagination began to imagine an alternative outcome to the accident. How on earth would she have coped with comforting Jamie and his gran if Buster had been killed? And how dreadful, she thought, if pedestrians and drivers had been hurt as well. Experiencing nagging doubts as to whether she had the strength needed to follow her father and brother into the same profession, Emma began to doze.

Some busy sparrows, eager for the day to begin, cheeped a welcome to it outside the window. Emma stirred in a dreamy state of half-sleep. Slowly, she began to open her eyes and leave sleep behind, focusing on Buster. He lay in exactly the same position – but once again, he had become motionless. Emma sat bolt upright. Buster looked limp and lifeless; his eyes half-closed. Her feet hardly touched the ground as Emma dashed to her parents' bedroom to wake her father.

When Mr Hodges had recovered from his daughter's attempt to wake him by persistently poking him in his shoulder, he reached for his dressing-gown and slippers and followed her downstairs.

"*Quick*, Dad! He's so still." As Emma opened the door and looked at the table where Buster lay, her heart sank. There didn't appear to be a spark of movement in the dog. She stared, tense and speechless, as her father listened with his stethoscope to Buster's heart. Tears began to well up in Emma's eyes. She tried to comfort herself with the thought that Buster had, at least, enjoyed some happy times with Jamie and his gran.

As Mr Hodges took the stethoscope from his ears he smiled. Confused by his expression, Emma moved towards him. "It's all right," he whispered. "He's asleep – that's all. And I'm not surprised, after all he's been through. Come and listen." Emma put the earpieces of the stethoscope in her ears, and very gently placed the other end of the instrument on Buster's chest. The steady, gentle thud reassured her. Her tears continued to form, but for a different reason now. She was so relieved – Buster was *alive*.

# Chapter 12

Hurriedly stuffing school books into her bag, while at the same time attempting to push a piece of toast into her mouth, Emma paused on her way to school when the telephone rang. It was Jamie, eager to hear the latest news on how Buster was faring. Emma told him of her false alarm that morning, laughing because she'd jumped to conclusions again, but she assured Jamie that his dog was sleeping soundly. Emma was pleased to hear Jamie had managed to convince his gran that she really hadn't been at all responsible for Buster running off. He sounded brighter and was looking forward to visiting later that day.

Throughout the day Emma's thoughts had often returned to Buster. She couldn't wait for her lessons to pass so that she could return home. At break-time she'd phoned home, and Sue had told her that Buster was fully awake. Jamie had visited, and his dog had greeted him with a feeble wag of his tail. Mr Hodges had explained that there were positive signs of improvement, even though Buster was probably feeling extremely uncomfortable from all the bruising, and from the fracture to his leg.

Emma's first sight of Buster, on arriving home from school, was encouraging. He appeared to sense her presence straight away. When she looked into the familiar, soft brown eyes, they seemed to be surprisingly bright. She ran her hand over his head. "Just keep this up, Buster. You're one amazing dog." Emma was pleased that Jack had moved Buster to a small back room where he lay quiet and cosy. Jack had made a good job of ensuring Buster was as comfortable as possible by providing a warm and spotlessly clean basket. It was lined with layers of disposable bedding and placed on the floor. There, Buster had drifted in and out of sleep throughout the day, except for frequent visits from the veterinary nurse to check on him. From time to time, Mr Hodges or Jack looked in to see how he was faring.

While Emma was making a fuss of Buster, Mr Hodges entered the room with an expression of exasperation on his face. "Taking care of Buster is a positive pleasure," he announced, "compared to another encounter with Casey." The tall man sighed.

"Surely not slow-worms again, Dad?" Emma enquired.

"No, something that poses *far* more of a threat to my reputation as a vet. Young Casey wants to work for me, or *help out*, as he put it, in his spare time." Mr Hodges made a face as though he was swallowing dreadful-tasting medicine. Emma tried to stifle a giggle. Her father took another look at Buster and read the observations his nurse had made throughout the day. He looked thoughtful, then said: "We'll just keep watching him at present. When he's more stable, I'll run some more tests to check that we still haven't overlooked anything, and everything is functioning properly."

# Chapter 13

Mr Hodges had hit upon an idea. Providing Jamie was in agreement, he felt Buster would benefit from being moved upstairs to be with the family. Buster now required more room to stretch stiffened limbs and make some effort to move about. Jamie had readily agreed to the suggestion, as usual embarrassed by the family's generosity. Mr Hodges pointed out that if Buster returned home, before he was completely well and free of the plaster cast, it could prove dangerous for Jamie's gran. A wobbly dog was a hazard she could do without.

* * *

"Hi boy! How you doing?" Jamie had made another visit to Buster. His dog turned to move in his basket. The big appealing eyes stared at Jamie and he wagged his tail.

"I just don't know how to begin to thank your dad for all he's done," said Jamie, as Emma made a fuss of his dog. She immediately sensed the boy's awkwardness once more, and changed the subject by asking:

"Any luck in finding work this week?"

"There are plenty of vacancies to be filled, but it's always the same reply when I tell them I need time off during the day to care for Gran." A look of determination spread across his gaunt, grey features. "I won't give up, though," he added.

Mr Hodges beamed with pleasure. Almost a fortnight had passed since the accident, and Buster had continued to gain in strength. Lots of rest had allowed swollen and bruised tissues to heal. It still seemed nothing short of a miracle to Mr Hodges that Buster had survived without some severe problems.

When Buster was moved upstairs he soon discovered he had the added attention of Mrs Hodges in the day. He grew to know that she would bring him tasty little tit-bits when she was preparing the family's meals. And Sue, whenever she had a moment to spare, climbed the stairs with Old Vic to visit him. The family had been pleased to discover that both Rosie their labrador, and Old Vic, had taken very well to Buster's presence in the house. On his first visit to see Buster, Old Vic had sniffed him before flopping down, contentedly, by his side. Rosie, after some initial surprise at finding a new addition to the family, soon became quite affectionate towards him. Sometimes her frequent enthusiasm had to be restrained. Her desire to clean Buster by licking his coat, at every opportunity, had made the injured dog apprehensive. On several occasions he'd tried to pull away from her. Emma managed to control the labrador with a firm grip on her collar and the words, "NO! Rosie!" repeated until the dog got the message. Still keen to return to grooming Buster, Rosie had sat obediently on the spot staring at him and panting. As Buster grew in strength he had demonstrated he was capable of grooming himself, despite contending with the plastered leg.

Buster's basket had been placed close to the window, which was open a little at the bottom. This meant he could savour the aromas drifting up from the street below. From where he lay, he was just about able to run his nose along the edge of the window-frame whenever the fish and chip shop along the road started to fry a fresh batch of fish, chicken, or burgers. He seemed content to lie there dozing most of the day, occasionally pricking up his ears at sounds in the street. At best, he could perform a few shaky steps from his basket around the room. It looked strange, because the plastered leg made any movement appear awkward. Emma knew the importance of getting him mobile as soon as possible. Just like a human body which has been injured, Buster's limbs needed to be exercised.

Buster soon settled into his new

surroundings with the family. He was quick to recognize the sound of Emma's voice when she came in from school and headed towards him. Rosie was nearly always close on her heels. Buster also sensed when Jamie was about to visit, almost every day. He often produced a dog chew for him from his pocket. Buster would lick his hand and feebly attempt to tug it from his grasp. Once it was secured between his teeth, he would chomp on it for ages until the tough, leathery strip became all soft and rubbery.

Buster's first real voyage from his basket happened one morning when the only person upstairs was Jack. He had invested in another guitar after the sad fate of the previous one, and sat in his room strumming on it. The one he'd purchased looked just as old and battered, showing evidence of someone having attempted to decorate it with pasted-on pictures of Spanish dancers. He'd assured everyone that it would produce good sounds after it had received some fine tuning. As far as Sue the receptionist was concerned, the chords drifting downstairs sounded much the same as the troublesome tom-cat that had been brought in that morning with an ear infection.

Buster lay in his basket, unable to avoid the strange, repetitive sounds of Jack practising on his guitar. Despite burrowing his head close to his body, to shut out the din, he still found the noise impossible to ignore. Temporary relief came when Jack went to make a coffee. But when he picked up the instrument again and launched into a mournful composition he'd been working on, Buster felt compelled to protest. Wobbling to a standing position, he managed to stagger from his basket and pad, slowly but purposefully, along the landing to Jack's room. Buster coped remarkably well; the stiff, plastered leg didn't appear to bother him. Outside Jack's room he stopped, wavering unsteadily in the doorway, just staring in as though trying to comprehend the sounds. Lifting his head in appreciation of a particularly difficult part in his composition, Jack suddenly noticed Buster standing there.

"Well done, Buster!" he called, congratulating the dog on the distance he had managed to walk. "You're getting better all the time. And developing a fine ear for good music, I see." Jack continued to strum tunelessly on the old guitar. He was pleased to have an audience, even if it was one injured dog with a plaster-cast on his leg. "Come on boy. Come and join me," said Jack, playing with renewed vigour until, without warning, Buster lifted his head and opened his mouth. A low, mournful howl followed, which Jack chose to take as a sign of appreciation.

"Not bad at all, Buster. I'm not sure what key you're in, but we make a pretty good sound together, I reckon. I might just try to record us." When Jack stopped playing, Buster's pathetic whining ceased. For a moment he stared blankly at Jack, before turning tail and wobbling back to the front room. Exhausted by his efforts, he flopped into his basket and, using his mouth, tugged his blanket over his head and slept.

\* \* \*

Over the evening meal, Jack explained how Buster had managed to walk to his room, lured from his basket by the haunting, animal-like rhythms of his guitar. Emma almost choked with laughter on her mouthful of pie, but Jack wasn't easily discouraged. He had given the incident some thought: MUSIC THERAPY FOR ANIMALS. He was certain his melodic playing had inspired Buster's confidence to walk. Emma continued to laugh out loud. "Can't you see, Jack – he was protesting!" But Mr Hodges looked thoughtful.

"You know, Jack – you might just be on to something there. Look into it."

"Oh, Dad!" protested Emma. "Please don't encourage him. Can you imagine it: Jack Hodges, heavily in demand by farmers the length and breadth of the country – all keen to employ him to get their herds on the move at milking time. Creatures everywhere responding to tapes of his awful strumming, like rats to the Pied Piper."

Jack's only response to his sister's jibes was to seize the opportunity of her talking to remove a beautifully roasted potato from her plate.

Emma couldn't wait to tell Jamie, later that evening, of Buster's successful trek from his basket. She also told him of Jack's claim, laughing as she recounted his theory. But Jamie seemed distracted; his face wore a worried, sombre expression. Emma guessed the reason. He had failed yet another job interview.

"Isn't it great," said Emma, attempting to cheer him up. "Buster is really on the mend." As Jamie knelt down and hugged his dog, fussing him for his brave effort, Mr Hodges walked into the room.

"Your Buster is a dog with remarkable reserves of strength, Jamie. I can admit to you now that when I first saw him lying in the road, I never thought he'd pull through." Buster extended a paw and placed it on Jamie's knee, patting him as a request for the boy to continue to fuss him.

# Chapter 14

"Well, Buster, it looks as though we've got the place to ourselves this Sunday afternoon," announced Emma. "I'm grounded until I've got my homework up to date, and everyone's gone out to do much more exciting things." Emma stood up. She had been brushing Buster with a soft brush and he appeared to be enjoying it. "I've got other plans, though," she added, mischievously. "First, I'm going to soak in a nice warm bath. Then, we'll settle down in front of the television with a tub of ice-cream. I might just let you have some, if you promise not to tell that I'm leaving history until tonight." Buster looked up at Emma from his basket by the window. A fresh gust of wind had sent the tantalizing aroma of spare-ribs, from the chip shop, wafting into the room. His mouth watered.

Emma filled the bath, adding a generous dribble of scented bath oil. She lay back and allowed herself to drift off into her favourite daydream: Emma Hodges on graduation day at veterinary college. The steam and heat in the bathroom soon made her drowsy and she realized it was time to leave her luxurious soak. She left her dream to the thunderous applause of fellow students and parents: she'd more than made the grade. Emma stepped out of the haze of steamy hot air, heady with the scent of the oil, and wrapped herself in her bathrobe. Around her head she swathed a towel in a turban-like arrangement. Still a little drowsy, she started to make her way across the landing to her bedroom, on wet, oily feet, which left little glistening puddles behind. As she was about to pass the top of the staircase, the pile of towelling on her head came loose and hung down over her face. For a few moments,

Emma groped about to gain control of it. Buster saw her from his basket, watching her actions with interest. Issuing a coarse, throaty bark, he stood up and staggered towards her. But Emma, without realizing, had moved very near to the top of the stairs.

Still struggling to free her face from the towel, she suddenly slipped on a wet patch and descended the stairs in a similar style to the way her brother Jack had fallen: bumping and tumbling her way to the bottom. As she hit the floor, one foot buckled beneath her, taking the full impact of her weight. She shrieked out in pain, but it was to an empty house. Only Buster responded by plodding to the top of the stairs where he stood looking down at her, his head on one side with a quizzical expression on his face.

Slowly and painfully she tried to assess any injuries by attempting to move each of her limbs in turn. When she moved, the foot twisted beneath her, and a sharp pain ran from the ankle along the length of her leg. It seemed to send ripples of pain through her whole body. She felt sick, but struggled to look up at Buster when she heard him bark. To her dismay, she saw that he stood with both front paws balanced on the very edge of the top stair. Fear clutched at her stomach.

"No, Buster! STAY!" she hollered, desperately afraid he would try to reach her. But Buster's reply was another enthusiastic bark and a wag of his tail. Seeing him poised above her, Emma was reminded of the moment he had stood at the side of the road, only seconds before he'd dashed into the traffic. She was petrified his next move would end in disaster.

Buster lifted his head and barked again. Showing an obvious desire to join Emma, he took his first tentative step down. "NO! GO BACK!" she shrieked, every muscle resonating with the painful effort of calling out. But Buster chose to take her words as encouragement, and continued to plod slowly down the steep flight of stairs. Emma averted her head and closed her eyes, anticipating, at any second, the impact of Buster's full weight landing on her. The pain in her ankle was increasing, but even that was easier to bear than watching the dog's descent of the stairs.

To Emma's amazement, the anticipated thud of Buster's body hitting the stairs – and then her – never happened. Cautiously, he had alighted from the last step and now stood over her, smothering the side of her face with warm licks.

"Thank goodness you're all right," Emma sobbed through her tears; a mixture of agony and relief. "What are we going to do, boy? It'll be ages before anyone arrives home." She made another attempt to move the injured foot from beneath her and, letting out a loud squeal, succeeded in tugging it free. She looked down with horror at an ankle that was rapidly swelling. Turning her head from side to side, she searched for inspiration to help her situation; perhaps something to aid her stand. Nothing came immediately into view until her gaze fell upon the telephone. It was only a little way off, but well out of reach in her predicament, although a thought had flashed across her mind. If she could interest Buster in tugging on the long cord, which hung down, he might just be able pull it towards her. Then she could dial for help. Anything was worth a try. Buster was still busily attempting to lick her face.

"Look, Buster!" Emma pointed with one hand to the phone. "FETCH!" For a moment he ceased licking, raised his head, then returned to her face. She managed to brush him aside, and several times repeated the command; her tone becoming more insistent. The urgency of her last attempt caused him to look up again, just as she had a brainwave. "Buster – remember your rope?" She pointed again. "ROPE – FETCH!" Emma had recalled a length of brightly coloured rope she'd bought for Buster in a pet shop. Despite him lying for long periods in his basket, he could still exercise with the aid of some gentle tugging with his teeth. Buster loved the game, happy to stay in his basket and pull on the rope for as long as possible.

The dog looked upstairs at the command, wondering if he should go in search of his piece of rope, but Emma persisted in repeating her command and pointing to the dangling cord, until he saw it. Eager to please, Buster barked, then seemed to understand that he was required to fetch it. The moment it was in his mouth, Emma praised him loudly: "Well done, boy!" she called. On wobbly legs Buster walked towards her, dragging the cord in his mouth. Another twinge of sharp pain shot up her leg, but she fought to keep Buster's interest focused on the cord. As he came closer, he started to growl excitedly. Emma had asked for 'the rope' – surely a game was in store? When the cord was stretched to its full length, the receiver toppled and fell to the floor. As Buster brought the cord within reach, Emma summoned all her strength and grabbed at it, dragging it and hauling in the receiver. Her persistence had paid off.

At the time, she thought it was possibly one of the most uncomfortable calls she had ever made. While she tried to press the buttons, she hoped would connect her to Sue's home, Buster, who was still keen for his game of tug, continued to shake the cord between his teeth. Emma fought to cling on to the receiver, while Buster dribbled over her, enjoying his game. After several attempts to dial the correct number, she managed to place a call to Sue. When Sue answered, she was confused at first by the sounds of a dog slavering and growling at the other end. She wondered if some practical joker, who knew she worked for a vet, imagined it would be funny to put a dog on the line. But when she thought she recognized Emma's muffled voice trying to make itself heard above Buster's growls, she enquired, "Em – is that *you*? You sound dreadful. Whatever is the matter?"

Emma hurriedly explained her situation. Within seconds of putting the telephone down, Sue had grabbed her set of keys to the clinic and left.

# Chapter 15

Sue arrived to find Emma stranded at the bottom of the stairs, with Buster still engaged in his game of tug with the telephone cord. The dog wondered why the game had suddenly come to an abrupt end when Sue took a firm grip of his collar. Her strong forearm swiftly guided him back upstairs and into his basket. When Sue shut the door, Buster just sat waiting patiently in his basket for Emma to return, and his game to continue.

The young doctor at the casualty department took care not to cause Emma any more pain than was necessary when he examined her ankle. But some was unavoidable – she winced several times. The slightest pressure on her ankle still made her feel very nauseous. Although the x-rays revealed no sign of a fracture, the severe sprain she'd received had caused her foot to swell up like a small football.

"Think of it this way, Em," said Sue, trying to cheer up Emma, while a nurse applied a support bandage, "at least you'll have some time off school. Your mum will make such a fuss of you."

"Think of it *this* way," replied Emma, making a glum face. "Me stuck upstairs with a throbbing ankle, and Jack strangling the strings of his horrible old guitar every spare moment."

"Don't worry," smiled Sue, "Jack is going to be a very busy young man next week. Your dad has plans for him. There's plenty of work to keep his hands occupied in the clinic."

Emma began to warm to the idea of doing very little except rest up with Buster close by for company.

\* \* \*

"You could have found something more original than falling downstairs – just like *me* – to get all the attention around here," teased Jack. Emma's parents had been shocked, on returning home, to find their daughter lying injured on the sofa. Both started to fuss over her. An enormous plateful of cheese on toast was hurriedly produced by her mother, and her father plumped up cushions to support her back and injured ankle. Even Buster lay in his basket, at one end of the sofa, looking up at her as though ready to obey her slightest command. Emma had praised him for ages on her return from the hospital. She could have been stranded and in pain for a lot longer, if it hadn't been for Buster's round-about way of fetching assistance.

"Listen, *you*," she said, poking Jack in the ribs with the end of a crutch the hospital had loaned her. "You were hardly injured when *you* fell. The family were there to rush to your side, too. If it hadn't been for brave Buster, I could have lain there for hours in agony."

Jack reached over to pat the dog's head and

Buster responded by wagging his tail. "All right, Sis. I confess: your injuries are *far* worse. How can I possibly be of service to you? Perhaps if I took a trip to the sweet shop for some magazines and choccies. Might that help take your mind off your suffering?"

With her mouth now far too full of delicious cheese on toast to reply, Emma just nodded her head in earnest agreement. The tablets to help ease her pain had already started to take effect and she was beginning to feel much more comfortable, but the opportunity of having her brother running around after her was too good to miss.

Emma's mother had telephoned Jamie to let him know of her daughter's accident. She'd told him of the part Buster had played in coming to her aid, even if he'd imagined it was all part of a game. Jamie was concerned and soon arrived to visit Emma. In his hands he held a small bunch of flowers for her, and a big rubbery toy bone for Buster to chew on. Jamie looked embarrassed as he placed the flowers in Emma's lap. But she soon put him at his ease.

"How lovely! I really could get used to being spoiled," she exclaimed.

Buster growled his appreciation at receiving the bone. Contented, he wrapped his jaws around the object and began to gnaw with enthusiasm.

"I can't believe he hobbled down the stairs to you, with that leg all plastered up. Shows how much stronger he's getting," said Jamie. He looked thoughtful, adding: "I think he must love living here with your family. I reckon he might never want to return to me and Gran. She misses him, you know?"

"Please don't think that way, Jamie. He's *your* dog and I'm sure that when he's fit again, he'll love being back in his real home," Emma replied.

Jamie tried to look as though he was convinced by her words, but he still had his doubts. "As soon as I can find some work, perhaps I'll be able to afford to build Buster a kennel in the backyard. I could get some plants and make the yard prettier for Gran as well. She can sit out there with Buster when she needs a change of scenery." His face had brightened as the idea took shape, and Emma voiced her enthusiasm. Mr Hodges, who had entered the room and caught the last words of Jamie's plan, was in agreement too.

"That sounds a great idea Jamie. There's plenty of spare scraps of wood in the shed out the back, if you want to help yourself and get started on that kennel. I'm sure Jack will give you a hand finding them."

Emma offered Jamie a slice of her cheese on toast as she munched on another piece herself. "I can think of a bit of wood that would be better suited to making a kennel," she muttered, indicating Jack's guitar propped up in a corner of the room.

Jack arrived back from the sweet shop laden with magazines and an enormous bar of chocolate he'd been unable to resist nibbling at one corner. Straight away, Emma volunteered him to assist Jamie in selecting timber scraps from the shed.

"Come on, Jamie. Let's leave Her Highness and see what's available." He whisked Jamie away to the sound of his father reminding him about a home visit later. A notoriously vicious cat, belonging to an old lady, needed attention. Mr Hodges reckoned that as Jack was used to working with much bigger animals, the cat should prove easy for him to handle, while he made his examination.

# Chapter 16

The venture into the cobweb-filled garden shed proved very productive for Jamie and provided an unlikely find for Jack. There were plenty of scraps of timber and even a length of roofing material. Jamie had more than enough to make a kennel for Buster. Sorting through one part of the shed, which looked as though it had remained uncleared for many years of junk from previous house owners, Jack unearthed an old banjo. He was thrilled with his find and anticipated spending hours cleaning and restoring the aged instrument.

As he sat at the kitchen table with Mr Hodges later that evening, Jack began the lengthy cleaning process the old banjo required. His work was a little hampered by a bandage around one hand. The home visit to the old lady's cat had resulted in a wrestling match between Jack and the animal, as he'd fought to restrain it. He looked up thoughtfully from some vigorous polishing.

"You know, Dad, that Jamie is all right. I always thought he looked so sullen, but most of it is because of this work thing; trying to find some sort of job that gives him time to care for his old gran. Can't we help him out there?"

Mr Hodges frowned. "I agree, it's a difficult situation. Although I'm not sure that there's anything *we* can do."

"But there is, Dad. I've been thinking about it," Jack continued. "You must admit, having me around for a while has been quite an asset to you over the past weeks?"

Mr Hodges smiled and raised his eyebrows. "Well, I have to confess, at the risk of adding to your already inflated opinion of yourself, that you've come in useful at times."

"That's just my point," replied Jack. "When I return to college at the end of next week, you're going to miss an extra pair of hands. What about taking on Jamie?"

Mr Hodges ran his hand across his face and looked thoughtful. "But Jack, *you* have a lot of experience with animals."

Jack was quick to answer: "Dad, it's been mostly the lifting and carrying that's helped you out. Jamie could do that – and probably a lot more, like checking supplies and organizing the rooms out the back. A part-time basis would suit you both."

Mr Hodges gave the idea some serious thought while Jack began to twang the strings of the banjo. The vet had to admit it: his son had come up with a good suggestion.

## Chapter 17

Buster hobbled from his basket over to the window and peered out. It was Friday afternoon. The traffic and the people going busily about their lives on the other side of the glass looked as grey and miserable as the weather. To Emma it seemed as though it had been raining all night and most of the day. Her first impressions of being able to lie around watching television and reading magazines, had soon lost their attraction. By the end of the week, boredom and frustration had set in.

While she rested her ankle, it no longer hurt, apart from the occasional twinge. Some of the swelling had gone down, but shades of blue, purple and even black showed above and below the bandage. Emma was hesistant about walking, even with crutches. Placing her foot down, she had to admit, had hurt the last time she'd tried it.

To enable her to keep up with school work, her teachers had sent assignments home. Even with this to occupy her time, the days seemed to drag by and she found it difficult to sleep at night, having had no exercise during the day. One thought had been nagging away at the back of her mind: Saturday morning clinic – and it was the next day. The prospect of missing it for just one week made Emma feel even more miserable.

"Dad's never going to let me help him while I can only limp around. It's no good Buster, I've got to start getting about on this ankle." Summoning all her strength, she hauled herself to a standing position. Very gradually she stretched the injured foot out in front. Hesitant at first, she carefully took a step and slowly released her full weight on to it. It felt strange; sort of numb from lack of use, but not too bad. Then she took another step and, to her surprise, although it was a little shaky, managed to support herself. Rapidly gaining in confidence, she smiled at Buster and took three more quick steps, like a baby who has just learned to walk. On the third, her ankle buckled and she yelped in pain, flopping down on to the sofa. Buster looked up at her cry. A little afraid, he shuffled to her side.

"Oh, Buster! At this rate, Dad's more likely to let *you* help out in the clinic tomorrow." Then, with an expression of complete determination on her face, Emma gritted her teeth and stood up again. This time, taking tiny, delicate steps like a catwalk model, she managed to manoeuvre herself from one side of the room to the other.

"*Ye-es!*" she shouted as she touched the far wall. "I'll be there at eight-thirty prompt tomorrow morning." Buster just hung his head on one side, confused by all the sudden strange activity.

Later that day, when Emma's parents entered the room, their daughter was ready for them.

Shocked, they watched her totter across the room. She was desperately hoping to convince them her ankle was healed. But Mr Hodges was quick to see through her forced smile as she gritted her teeth in obvious discomfort. Her ankle was beginning to hurt after all the activity that afternoon.

"Sorry Emma – I'm not convinced. I know what your little performance is all about. You're trying to impress on me how you're suddenly fit enough for clinic tomorrow. I'm sorry, but you'll have to put that idea out of your mind; your ankle is still very weak. Anyway, we can't have you tripping over dogs, and cat baskets. The place will end up littered with casualties."

Emma scowled and sank into an armchair, her arms crossed over her chest. She knew it was pointless to argue with her father. Mr Hodges looked at her with pity; he knew how important Saturday morning surgery was to his daughter. He reflected for a few moments, deciding that she had, after all, been very patient sitting alone for days. He was prepared to offer a compromise: she could stay in reception with Sue and answer the telephone for the last hour of morning surgery. But this was only if she promised to sit still and rest her leg on a chair. Perhaps the change of scenery would do her good. Emma was grateful for her father's suggestion. Answering the telephone and watching the animals come in was certainly better than nothing, she concluded.

When Jamie called in the evening, he was greeted by good news. Mr Hodges had examined Buster that day. He was satisfied with his progress. Buster had enjoyed the attention he'd received from Emma during her week of rest at home but, like her, he was showing signs of wanting to move around more. Mr Hodges found this very encouraging, but still envisaged that Buster should continue to stay with them until the plaster was off, and the leg proved to be completely healed.

Jamie was pleased to tell them how he had spent the afternoon thumping away with a hammer until he'd produced a sturdy kennel for Buster. His own skill had amazed him. He'd put the finishing touches to the kennel by carving Buster's name into a little plaque, and carefully attaching it to the front. Jamie imagined Buster snoozing in the shade of the kennel on a summer's day, while his gran sat in the tiny backyard. He would start to brighten it up with plants and hanging baskets – just as soon as he'd found some work to pay for them.

Buster sat looking up at Jamie, anticipating the dog-chew he could smell in the boy's pocket. When it was produced, Buster grabbed it neatly between his teeth and padded back to his basket. Rosie had trotted in from the kitchen at the now familiar presence of Jamie in the house. She, too, was often treated to a dog-chew by him. She sat wagging her tail and looking up expectantly, until he put his hand in his pocket and pulled out a strip for her. Having secured it in her mouth, Rosie lost all interest in Jamie and sank down next to Buster to enjoy some communal chomping.

"I just wish there was some way I could

show you how grateful I am for everything you've done for him," said Jamie, watching his dog gnawing contentedly on the leathery strip. "I mean – you've healed him, fed him, and cared for him. It's really put Gran's mind at rest too."

Mr Hodges turned to Jamie and smiled. "Well, there is *something* you could do," he said, "but you'll probably need to think about it. You could always come and work for me. As my son pointed out, I could do with some extra help, and you need employment."

Emma squealed, "Dad – that's *brilliant!*"

For a boy who rarely smiled, Jamie's face suddenly lit up the room like the sun emerging from clouds on a dismal day. Then, just as quickly, the smile disappeared.

"There's nothing I'd rather do, Mr Hodges, but I bet the sort of hours I can work are very different from the ones you have in mind."

"Don't worry, Jamie, I know all about your gran's needs. Just as long as you're able to lift and carry – and perhaps organize a few supplies and deliveries – you can fit the hours around caring for her."

# Chapter 18

Jack was reeling from the sisterly attention he was receiving from Emma. "You are simply the *best* brother, and the most *talented* musician I have ever known," she announced at breakfast the next morning. Fortunately, Jack couldn't see her fingers crossed behind her back for the last part of the statement.

Jack spluttered cornflakes across the table, amazed by his sister's sudden outburst. "What on *earth* have I done to justify this – even though your remarks just happen to be true?"

"Dad told me it was your idea to give Jamie a job – and for that – I am eternally indebted to you," Emma replied.

"Hmm," mused Jack. "Could be interesting. But I think I'll settle for repeats of the best musician bit – on the hour – for the rest of my stay," he chuckled.

Mr Hodges suggested it would be a good idea if Jamie attended the clinic that morning, so he could see how things worked. Sue would be on hand to advise him and designate any jobs. That way he could feel his way around. It would be good preparation for when he started the following week.

"You're going to do just fine, Jamie," said Sue. "I can tell. Old Vic has taken to you and that's always a good sign." The friendly receptionist soon put Jamie at his ease, while her aged dog licked his hand. And, within an hour, Jamie had already begun to prove her right. He was very efficient and quick to learn the way things were run. Not only did he carry out any requests competently, but he was ready to recognize where he could be of immediate assistance. When a large quantity of stores were delivered, he was soon at the driver's side helping him carry the boxes through to the storeroom out the back. By the end of the morning Jamie had tidied and stacked all the new supplies. He had even found time to make some new labels for the shelves where they were stored. It was strange the way Buster seemed to sense Jamie's presence as he worked downstairs. He wagged his tail whenever he heard the boy's voice drifting upwards.

As if on cue, with exactly one hour to go before the close of morning surgery, Emma appeared in reception. Her mother had helped her to walk down the stairs. Eagerly, she squeezed in next to Sue, lifted her leg on to a chair to rest it, and cheerfully announced: "Remember? Dad promised I could answer the phone for the last hour."

Sue pulled a miserable face. "How very kind of him. I would imagine that sets me free to catch up on this mound of paperwork. Yuk!" She indicated a pile of files and papers balanced precariously on one side of her desk. It was her least favourite part of the job. Talking to the clients and their animals was what she liked best.

110

Emma looked around the waiting area at the few remaining pets and their owners. Her attention was taken by a young woman who sat very sedately balancing a luxurious cat basket on her lap. It housed a beautiful grey and white cat with long soft fur. Emma could just make out the exquisite features of the animal as it sat in the dark recess of the basket. From its collar dangled an ornate, golden pendant which sported a brilliant green gem. Engraved on it in elaborate script was the name: Geraldine.

Next to Geraldine and her owner sat an anxious-faced boy with a straw-filled box. Something scratched around inside it, making a grating sound. From the expression on the face of Geraldine's owner, the noise obviously made her more than a little apprehensive. Just what kind of creature lurked within? Did it possess nails, a beak or claws? The noise was so persistent. Emma took a card bearing details of the next patient her father was due to see. They revealed the contents of the box to be a one-year-old guinea-pig named Jason who, for some reason, wasn't eating. When the boy and his pet were called into Mr Hodges' surgery, Geraldine's owner breathed a sigh of relief, but there was only temporary respite for her. She was soon made uneasy again. A young girl sitting the other side of her suddenly asked if she would like to see her pet giant snail. Unfortunately it was suffering with some "fungusy stuff". This was too much for Geraldine's owner to bear, and with a look of disgust, tinged with nausea, she made her excuses and moved to a seat on the opposite side of the room.

Emma loved being back downstairs. The atmosphere of pets and their owners, and the change of scenery was doing her a power of good. She spent the rest of the morning surgery answering the telephone with cheerful enthusiasm.

It seemed to Emma as though she had hardly been downstairs any time at all when Sue showed out the last patient for the morning, and turned the sign on the door to CLOSED. Just as the door shut, and Sue turned to go back to her desk, a small figure appeared and banged on the door. Sue instantly recognized the outline through the glass.

"Oh no!" she exclaimed, reaching to unlock the door. "And I thought we were going to make it through a whole week without a visit from Casey. What can he possibly have in that box? There isn't much left in the animal kingdom that he hasn't brought through the door at some time. Could it be electric eels, or perhaps a pygmy shrew, this time?"

"Casey," Emma called, unable to resist the boy's ready smile, but cautioning him all the same. "Don't say you haven't been warned. Dad has told you often enough about acquiring more creatures. I think it's best if you just turn around and take whatever is inside the box, back to the person you got it from – unless of course there's something seriously wrong with it – or them?"

Casey crossed to where Emma sat. His confident smile told the world he was completely in the clear this time. "But it's not mine," he stated. "Your dad won't be angry, because what's in here doesn't belong to *me*." Emma looked puzzled. Then, with pride, Casey handed it to her, announcing: "This is a present for you. I heard about your accident and wanted to give you something really special as a get-well gift."

Emma ran her hand through her hair and turned to look at Sue, who was equally disarmed. It was impossible to stay angry with the boy for long. He genuinely sought to please. Thrusting the box into her hands, Casey stood back waiting for approval of his choice. Emma wondered what she could possibly do but accept his gift. Cautiously lifting the lid, just in case Hubert the tarantula was about to put in another appearance, she peered in. Two shiny, dark eyes and a delicately whiskered pink nose rose to meet her. She opened the box wider and saw the sweetest young golden hamster, keen to explore its surroundings. Emma looked back at the eager face of the young boy.

"Knew you'd like it. I swapped my football

scarf and half my best collection of football cards for it."

"Casey," Emma replied, "this is probably the most beautiful present anyone has ever given me, but you really mustn't think of animals as things to be given away or swapped. They're living creatures and need to be respected and cared for. If someone is going to own a pet, they need to know just what's involved in keeping it beforehand."

Casey looked thoughtful, then nodded his head in agreement. While Emma stood stroking the little hamster, Jamie brought Buster into the waiting room. Mr Hodges had suggested taking the dog into the little back garden for a longer spell of fresh air than the short, but necessary, visits for which he was taken every day.

"That dog's plaster cast on his leg," enquired Casey with interest, "I don't suppose I could sign my name on it, could I? There's a girl at school with a cast on her arm. It's covered in names and drawings."

Emma immediately declined Casey's request. Not to be discouraged, the young boy's parting remark was to promise he would return with something for Buster – something he would really like. Emma was quick to reply that as long as the "something" wasn't a *live* something, it would probably be acceptable. She was relieved to hear Casey intended to bring Buster a ball he'd found in the park. Buster could make good use of it when his leg was mended.

As Sue cooed over the little hamster, Emma reached to answer the phone. At the other end the voice of a young woman sounded distraught.

"My little kitten has been *so* sick. Please can the vet come to my home. The poor thing suddenly became very weak." In calm, sympathetic tones Emma took the young woman's address and some more details about the kitten. Then she assured her that the vet would be with her very soon.

A busy morning at Handley Road clinic had just ended, but for Mr Hodges and his family, another case had just presented itself.

\* \* \*

Buster stood in the little back garden raising his head to inhale all the exciting aromas. The world smelled good to him. His keen nostrils could detect so many special scents. He turned and looked back at Jamie, as though seeking permission to wander further up the path. Jamie encouraged him to move, watching his dog's progress along the little garden. The time would soon come when the tan mongrel dog with the big brown eyes would be running free again. But before that could happen, Jamie was determined that Buster would attend dog obedience classes. Never, he vowed, as his dog padded back up the path to him, a stick clenched between his teeth, eager for a game of tug, would Buster wander off near roads and traffic again.